Do Not EVER Be a Babysitter!

by Michaela Muntean

illustrated by Pascal Lemaître

Scholastic Press / New York

For Esme and Adrien — thank you for helping me write this book!   — M.M.

To all the brave babysitters everywhere.   — P.L.

10 9 8 7 6 5 4 3 2 1   20 21 22 23 24 • Printed in Malaysia   108 • First edition, April 2020

Pascal Lemaître's artwork was created using pen and ink, colored in Adobe Photoshop. • The text type was set in Chauncey Decaf Medium. • The display type was set in Coop Heavy. • The book was printed on 130 gsm Lumisilk Matt Art Paper and bound at Tien Wah Press. • Production was overseen by Catherine Weening. • Manufacturing was supervised by Shannon Rice. • The book was art directed and designed by Marijka Kostiw, and edited by Tracy Mack.

Oh, hello. I don't know why you're here, but if you're looking for a babysitter, you are out of luck.

or WASHING
instructions . . .

or a
REPAIR manual?

No? Sigh.

I told my sister I would babysit,
but I had no idea children could be
so LOUD and MESSY!

Hmmmm . . .
she did leave a list. Maybe you can help
me understand it.

It starts with
PLAYTIME.

Home Sweet Home.

HOW TO KEEP THEM HAPPY
1 PLAYTIME
2 SNACK TIME
3 STORY TIME
4 NAP TIME

Then **SNACK TIME.**

Oh, I DO like snacks. A spoonful of caviar or some Limburger cheese would just hit the spot.

And then **STORY TIME.**

Wonderful idea! What could be better than
curling up with a good book?

And finally **NAP TIME.**

I certainly COULD use a nap.
Taking care of children is EXHAUSTING.

Oh NO!
No, NO, NO, NO . . .
please DO NOT touch that . . .
or open that . . .
or climb on that . . .
or jump on that . . .
or crawl under
or over or into that!

So far, you haven't been much help, have you?
Okay, I'll give you another chance.
Tell me if these are GOOD or BAD ideas
for keeping children entertained:

1. Let them sort socks and fold underwear. Doing laundry can be LOADS of fun.

2. Have them scrub the tub and toilet.

3. Let them vacuum under the beds and behind the sofa.

4. Take them outside to run around.

Would you PLAY with us?

How about a SNACK?

Can you please READ us a story?

Maybe being a babysitter isn't so bad after all.

TO BE (OR NOT TO BE) A BABYSITTER

Taking care of children is _____.

It's true children can be noisy and messy,
but they can also be _____.

The best thing any babysitter can do is
_____.

If a babysitter gets tired or crabby, give
that babysitter a _____.

The best babysitter I know is _____.